A boy's guide to school

Sharon Witt

Wiseguys® – A Boy's Guide to School
Book 2 in the Wise Guys series

Published by Collective Wisdom Publications Pty Ltd
PO Box 150
Mt Evelyn Victoria 3796
www.sharonwitt.com.au

ISBN: 978-0-6483732-3-0

A catalogue record for this
work is available from the
National Library of Australia

Design and cartoons: Ivan Smith, Communiqué Graphics, Lilydale
Printed in Australia by Openbook Howden

This book belongs to an

INCREDIBLE young man...

....

Inside

BULLYING

GETTING TO KNOW YOUR TEACHER

SCHOOL DAYS

HOMEWORK

WHAT TO DO IF... (Some common questions at school)

DEVICES AND THE INTERNET

REST AND PLAY TIME

Hey there
a message from me

WELCOME to WiseGuys. I am really happy that you have picked up this book and either having a read yourself, or reading along with a parent or caregiver.

This book has been written especially to help you in the years that you will be moving through primary school. School can be a great time of learning new things, making friends, getting to know new teachers, playing lots of games, taking on **NEW CHALLENGES**, and learning to be part of a community.

School can also be tricky sometimes. Perhaps you feel a bit **NERVOUS** when you are faced with new situations. Or maybe, making new friends is tough for you. You may find it a little bit scary to be away from home during the day and you find yourself missing your parents.

You may notice that I have included a wonderful, amazing co-author in this book. I am very excited to introduce you soon to **BEN**, who will also offer some helpful advice along the way as well. ☺

Hopefully you will feel a **LOT** better after reading through this book. You may read it many times over as you move through primary school. Sometimes, you might simply pick up a chapter in the book to help you through a particular problem or challenge you face.

Just remember, there are **MANY** people that are here to help you through your primary school years. You are never alone.

You are **AWESOME**.

Happy reading!

Sharon

Introducing my helpful co-author!

Meet Ben

Hey guys! My name is Ben, and I am 9 years old and in Grade 3 this year at school. I am excited to be a part of this book and give you some **HELPFUL ADVICE** for school. Here is a little more about me.

Favourite hobbies

I really enjoy riding my bike, and working on adding new things to it. I also like playing billiards downstairs at my house, and playing laser tag with my step-dad. In summer I like going in my pool. I also really enjoy cooking yummy meals like home-made butter chicken, and tacos. I also enjoy baking cinnamon and banana muffins and home-made chocolate mousse with my grandma. I have even included my favourite banana muffin recipe for you in this book. ☺

Best thing I like about school

At school I really enjoy playing with my friends. I like going on the computers in the classroom for the program 'Reading Express.' I enjoy sport the most, and love doing the fitness test (Beep test). I also love it when my teacher plays the Kahoot game during Italian class.

Best memory so far of primary school

My favourite memory so far is going on a school excursion to a brussel sprout farm. We got to taste brussel sprout soup, which was actually very tasty. I don't normally like to eat brussel sprouts on their own.

Favourite food

My favourites foods are butter chicken and bolognaise with penne pasta.

Favourite subject

I enjoy writing, especially narratives. I also like Italian, Sport, and Global Studies which involves us learning about countries, nature and animals.

Best holiday I've been on

I've only travelled to South Australia so far. My favourite memory was visiting the beach and riding on a giant ferris wheel. Mum was screaming the entire time we were on it. Afterwards, I had a triple scoop ice-cream with chocolate, strawberry and pistachio scoops.

Favourite television program

My favourite television show is called *Deadly Dinosaurs*. You learn facts about dinosaurs – how long they lived for, how strong each species was, and what they ate.

If I were an animal, I'd like to be...

I would choose to be a bird so that I could fly.

A NEW ADVENTURE BEGINS

The school year awaits you
A GREAT place to be
Who will you meet?
Who will you see?
Whatever you make of it
You get to decide
To LEARN and DISCOVER
You're in for a ride!
Make sure you ask QUESTIONS
Be adventurous and SEEK
To DISCOVER new things
Every day, every week
This is your NEW adventure
Yes, it is true
To LEARN all you can
This year is for you

What are you most looking forward to at school this year?

I AM EXCITED TO LEARN NEW THINGS.

Starting
School

Starting school

I still remember my very first day of primary school. I was exactly four years and nine months old and I was **VERY** ready to begin the new adventure. I couldn't wait to meet my first teacher, go and buy my first ever school bag, lunch box, and pencil case. I also knew that some of my friends from kindergarten would also be joining me at my new school. I was so excited to be spending five days in a row with a whole bunch of **FRIENDS**. Sounded exciting to me – and it was.

For the most part, my seven years at primary school were very happy, full of laughter, lots of learning and new adventures. My best memories were of playing with friends outside at recess, wearing my favourite stripy coloured tights (I was **VERY** cool!), making many artistic creations, including a panelled window made from different coloured cellophane, and of course, day trips to many places, including the zoo and the museum.

If you are about to start school for the very first time, you may be feeling **EXCITED**, or a bit **NERVOUS** (like you have one thousand butterflies in your tummy!). Maybe worried about what it will be like, or very happy and prepared

because you have been waiting for this moment for what seems like a **LONG** time.

Perhaps you are **WORRIED** about getting to know lots of new people, scared that other students might not talk to you, or who will you play with at recess.

But try not to worry. **EVERYONE** has to begin school at some stage; your mum, dad, grandma, grandpa, aunts and uncles, or your big sister or brother have **ALL** started school at some point.

And guess what?

They got through it!

And you know another thing about school? The more you go to school, the more **FAMILIAR** it becomes, and the more comfortable you will be.

'My Favourite thing about being in school is having lots of friends who aren't mean to you.'

No name or age

'The best thing about school is playing with my friends.'

Ethan, aged 10

'My favourite thing about being in school is recess and lunchtime. Also, lessons that are fun such as literacy, creative writing, science and technology.'

Rocco, aged 11

'That I don't need to worry about lots of homework.'

Ben, aged 9

'I like Primary school because I have lots of friends to play with.'

Oscar, aged 9

'The best thing about Primary school is learning about new things and having fun with my friends.'

Judah, aged 10

'My favourite thing about being in school is getting to see and play with my friends. I am lucky that I have a couple of good friends who are good to talk to and play with. I also love learning new things, especially art and P.E.'

Leo, aged 11

'My favourite thing about school is meeting new friends each year.'

Alex, aged 10

Coping with change

CHANGE sometimes causes us to worry a bit. Perhaps you have already experienced changes in your life already.

You might have:

- Moved house
- Changed schools
- Had a new baby join your family
- A change in your family circumstances
- Moved interstate
- Lost a pet

However you are feeling right now, remember that you have lots of **SUPPORT** to help you start school well and settle in comfortably. You don't have to worry about learning everything straight away either! You will have plenty of time to learn things like where the toilets are, where the playground is, what time playtime and lunch are, and what your day will look like. Your teachers are there to **HELP YOU**, listen to your questions, and will answer any questions you have along the way.

Don't forget! It's more than okay to **ASK QUESTIONS**.

Over your many years at school, you will learn to ask **MANY** questions. That's how you learn new things.

The good news is, you are **NEVER ALONE**.

There are always helpful adults (your parents or caregiver) who will be in your life every step of the way.

Are you ready to find out more about what to expect at school?

Okay, then let's **READ AHEAD!**

Beginning a new school year

Perhaps you are about to begin your very **FIRST** year at school (sometimes known as Prep, Reception or Foundation) depending on where you live. Or maybe you have already been at school for a year or more.

However, each year is a new beginning at school. Over the summer break, you will have quite a few weeks off school.

This could be anywhere from five to seven weeks depending on which school you attend.

It is a good thing to have a **BREAK** from school at the end of the year. You have worked hard and used your **BRAIN** a lot to learn many new things.

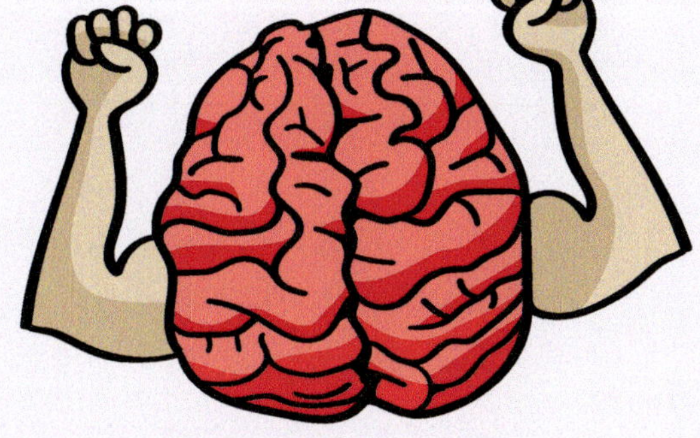

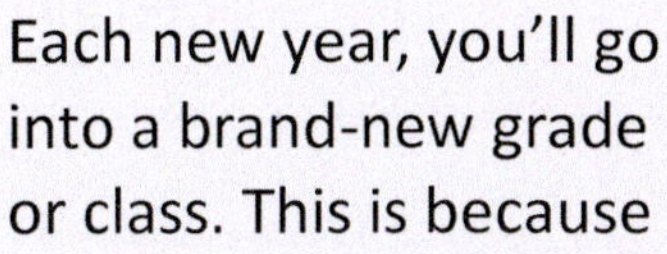

Each new year, you'll go into a brand-new grade or class. This is because you are a year older now. You may be in a class with some of your friends from last year, and you'll also have new children join your class.

It's a good thing to have new classmates because this is a wonderful opportunity to get to know **NEW FRIENDS**.

You might be feeling a bit excited about beginning a new year at school and seeing your friends again. You'll most likely have a **NEW TEACHER** and are looking forward to being in their class.

Or you may be feeling **NERVOUS**, **WORRIED** or a little bit unsure about what to expect when you go back to school. Perhaps you didn't have the best experience at school last year and didn't find your days easy or enjoyable.

If that is the case, I want you to think about this for a moment.

You have a brand-new, never-to-be-repeated year ahead of you.

Write here about your first day of school...

Write here about a favourite day of school...

A brand-new beginning

Last year has come and gone, and guess what? You got through it. If last year wasn't the best for you, try not to go into this new school year worrying about what has already gone.

You can begin a BRAND-NEW year with a FRESH ATTITUDE.

Imagine that it is going to be a great year at school. You are going to do your VERY BEST.

Perhaps you found it difficult to pay attention in class last year, or you found yourself being told to stop interrupting in class.

Maybe that left you feeling UPSET or FRUSTRATED.

You can make a decision to sit at the front of the class, if possible, and decide to practise LISTENING more to your teacher and using eye contact.

Maybe you found it difficult to learn your spelling words, or challenging to practise your reading. That is okay! Plenty of children find different things at school tricky.

It may take some time for these things to become EASIER for you.

What I want you to do, as you begin a new year, is to FOCUS on the things that you CAN do already. For example, maybe you are an ENCOURAGING friend to others.

Or perhaps you are always very HELPFUL to your teacher, asking if there's anything you can do to help at the end of a class.

Do you keep your books and pencils neat and tidy? Do you enjoy creating pieces of art? Maybe you find working with numbers easier than other students.

The point is, focus on the things that you CAN DO, rather than the things that feel CHALLENGING.

We ALL have things that are harder for us than others. For example, I'm not brilliant at understanding maths, but I LOVE to write, and I REALLY enjoy talking with and making new friends.

So put on a BIG SMILE! Have a POSITIVE attitude, and let's get into it. ☺

Settling into a new school

If you have moved house recently or have had to move schools for any other reason, it can be **SCARY** to start again at a new school. We can feel **NERVOUS** or **WORRIED** – even excited – because we are **UNSURE** about what to expect.

> **'Will I make new friends easily?'**
> **'Will I like my teachers, and will they like me?'**
> **'Will I be able to find my way around the new school?'**
> **'What if the work is much harder than I'm used to?'**

These are all **NORMAL** questions to ponder when experiencing such a change.

Perhaps you know someone who already attends that school. Ask your parents or caregiver to help organise a time to catch up with them. You might be able to ask your friend some questions about your new school.

Ben says...

I changed schools halfway through Grade 1. I felt very nervous before I started at my new school. Because it was halfway through the school year, I didn't go to orientation. I was a little worried that I would have no one to talk to. On the first day I arrived at my new school, halfway through the day I had already made two brand new friends – Hassan, and Josh. Then three days later, our assistant principal showed me all around the school. He told me that if I ever felt like I was lost, to not worry – there would always be someone who could help me.

Other children introduced themselves to me first, which helped. They were really kind. At snack time, we played a game of tiggy together on the grass area. After that, I felt happy and included at school.

Orientation Day

Before you begin attending school every day, you will most likely go and have a visit at your new school for a half or full day. This will probably happen towards the end of the year before you start, leading up to the big summer holidays.

This is called **ORIENTATION**. On this day, you will meet your teacher, make some new friends who are most likely going to be in your class next year, and familiarise yourself with the school grounds. Sometimes when we are experiencing something brand new, for the first time, we can feel a little nervous. We may not know what to expect. (Hopefully this book helps. ☺) When we actually go and visit a new place or go with someone we trust, it can help us feel better about going the next time because it won't be so new each time.

Here are some things you might do on Orientation Day:

- Meet your teacher that you'll have next year
- Play some games
- Practise writing your name
- Play in the playground
- Listen to a story
- Go for a tour of the Primary School
- Meet new friends
- Find out where you will put your school bag when you begin school
- Do some drawing or painting
- Eat your food

Celebrate who you are!

During your many years at school, you will discover that you have many **UNIQUE** qualities that make you who you are! You will also meet many others who have similar qualities to you, and others who are **DIFFERENT** to you. This is a good thing.

Imagine if we all had the same strengths? For example, if every student had strong leadership skills, it could make it very interesting if you were working on a group project together. Or if everyone was highly skilled in artwork, but no one could come up with exciting ideas, that could also be troublesome.

If you have thoughts and opinions about topics you feel strongly about – speak up! The world needs to hear your voice.

If you have strong ideas and would like to share these, develop your leadership skills. The world needs strong guys just like you who can show leadership in so many areas of life.

If you love to create, write, paint, draw or make up scripts to perform to others – celebrate these talents! The world needs you too ☺.

Let's Get Organised

Getting prepared!

What you'll need for school

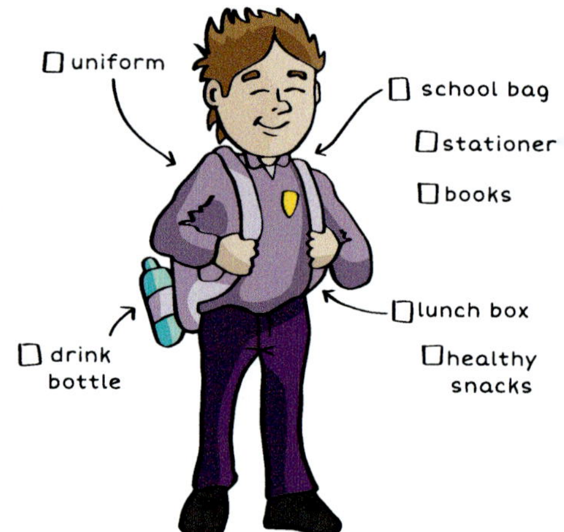

Your parents or caregiver will receive a notice from your new school that will explain all the items you will need to bring on your first day. Don't worry about this. They will help you get these **ORGANISED** and **LABELLED** so you're ready to start.

So let's take a look at some of the items you may need for your very first day at school:

- School bag
- Stationery (books, pencil case)
- Lunch or healthy snacks (you may only attend half a day for the first week)
- Drink bottle
- Uniform

(Some primary schools have a **UNIFORM** and as part of this, they have a special school bag that has the school colours and logo on it.)

If you have already been at school before now, you may still have a pretty good school bag from last year. If not, you can have fun choosing a brand new one for the new school year. Many schools, however, have a school bag as part of their uniform, and you'll use the same one as everyone else. Make sure that you don't put too many books and other items in your bag – you need to ensure there isn't too much weight on your back and shoulders.

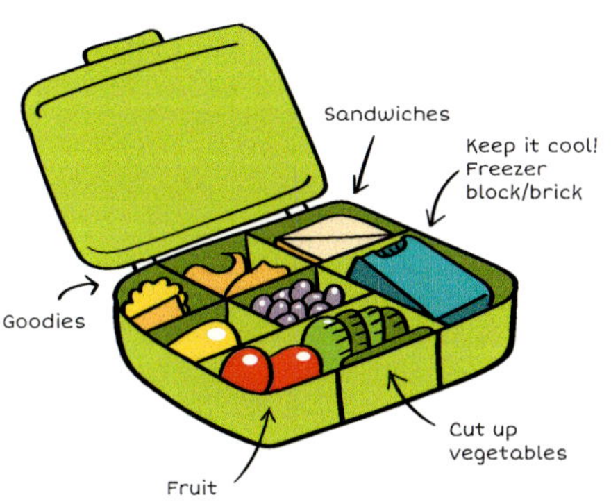

Lunch box

Choose a lunch box with a few different compartments if possible. This will help you to be able to include a variety of different foods such as fruit, cut-up vegetables, dips and sandwiches to keep your body and brain **WELL FED** throughout the school day.

A lunch box that also has a place to hold a small **FREEZER BRICK** is very helpful. That way, your lunch box will stay nice and cool through the warmer months.

Water bottle

You need to drink **LOTS** of water throughout the day to keep your mind and body active and working properly. If you don't like the taste of plain water too much, try adding a few drops of **LEMON** to your water (not cordial!). Avoid adding any sugary drinks to your water bottle – H_2O is the way to go!

Make sure you refill it during the day.

TOP TIP

If you know ahead of time that tomorrow is going to be very warm at school, fill your water bottle up to the ¾ mark and no more (as water expands when frozen) and store it in the freezer overnight. That way, during the day as it begins to defrost, you'll have a nice, cold, icy drink.

You can also place the cold water bottle on the back of your neck to cool yourself down when outside playing.

School books

You will probably have quite a few school books at home that may need COVERING before you begin the new school year. Some boys like the plain contact over their books (which protects your books in case they get wet or have something spilt on them).

Others prefer to choose some bright or patterned contact, or SPECIAL book covers to personalise their books. For example, you may love popstars or specific cartoon characters, and might be able to find some book covers that have those images. You might even like to find some images of your favourite sports stars or images you like. It may be worth checking with your school if they are happy for you to personalise your books with pictures and patterns (most teachers are ☺).

Don't try and cover your books in contact yourself. It is more difficult than you may realise. You might need a parent or another helpful adult to handle this job!

TOP TIP

LABEL EVERYTHING!!!!

Your name is **YOUR OWN**, and it is important to put your name on **EVERYTHING** that you are going to bring to school with you. As careful as you may be, things do go missing, and other students may borrow items without telling you (it happens ☹.)

You can ask a helpful adult to write your full name on all of your school items – or you may even purchase some vinyl name stickers online that come in packets. Usually, there are lots of name stickers that you can attach to all your things.

Stationery

Many schools will provide you with a list of the items you will need to use at school in the classroom, such as pencils, erasers, textas, rulers, etc.

Some schools on the other hand, will send home a **STATIONERY LIST** with items that your parents or caregivers will need to purchase for you.

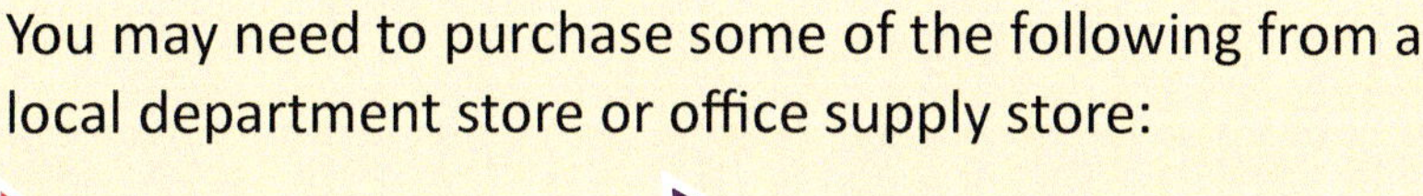

You may need to purchase some of the following from a local department store or office supply store:

- Pencil case
- Pencil sharpener
- Eraser
- Coloured pencils
- Grey lead pencils
- Coloured textas
- Scissors
- Glue stick
- Ruler

Sun hat

Once again, this may already be part of your school uniform, depending on which primary school you are attending. Some schools **EXPECT** you to bring your own broad brim hat with you to school each day (or keep it in a special place in your classroom, such as your locker or tub). It is **VERY** important that you make sure you are being **SUN SMART** at school when you are playing outside and protect your head from the sun's harmful UV rays.

Uniform

Many schools will have a **UNIFORM** that all students are required to wear. If this is not your first year at school, you could try on last years' school uniform a few weeks before school goes back. If it's your very first year at school, make sure that you take the time to try on your brand-new uniform about two weeks before you begin school – just in case you've grown a bit more over the holidays. ☺

Take care of your uniform!

When you get home from school, if your school uniform is still clean, make sure you **HANG IT UP** in your wardrobe or **FOLD IT NEATLY** and put it in your drawer or on the end of your bed.

Don't dump your clothes on your bedroom floor. If they are dirty, pop your uniform in your dirty clothes basket or in the laundry basket.

School shoes

Many schools will require you to have special school shoes (often black) to go with your uniform. These shoes can be purchased from many different stores. You will most likely go with a parent or caregiver and try them on to make sure they are **COMFORTABLE**, and that you have room to grow! It's not a good idea to get your school shoes too soon.

Some schools allow you to wear comfy sneakers or runners for school. As long as you can put your own shoes on and take them off yourself, you will be fine.

If you have shoes with **LACES**, you need to ask a helpful adult to teach you how to tie your own shoelaces. This will take some practice to get it right, but you'll pick it up in no time.

Some children find it easier to wear school shoes with **VELCRO**, which may make it easier for you to put on and remove your own shows.

PRACTISE wearing your school shoes at home in the couple of weeks **BEFORE** you start school, especially if you are wearing shoes specifically fitted for you. This is because it may take your shoes some time to wear in properly. (They can feel a bit hard at first before they soften.) Then, if any adjustments need to be made, your parents can do this before you start school.

Checklist for school supplies

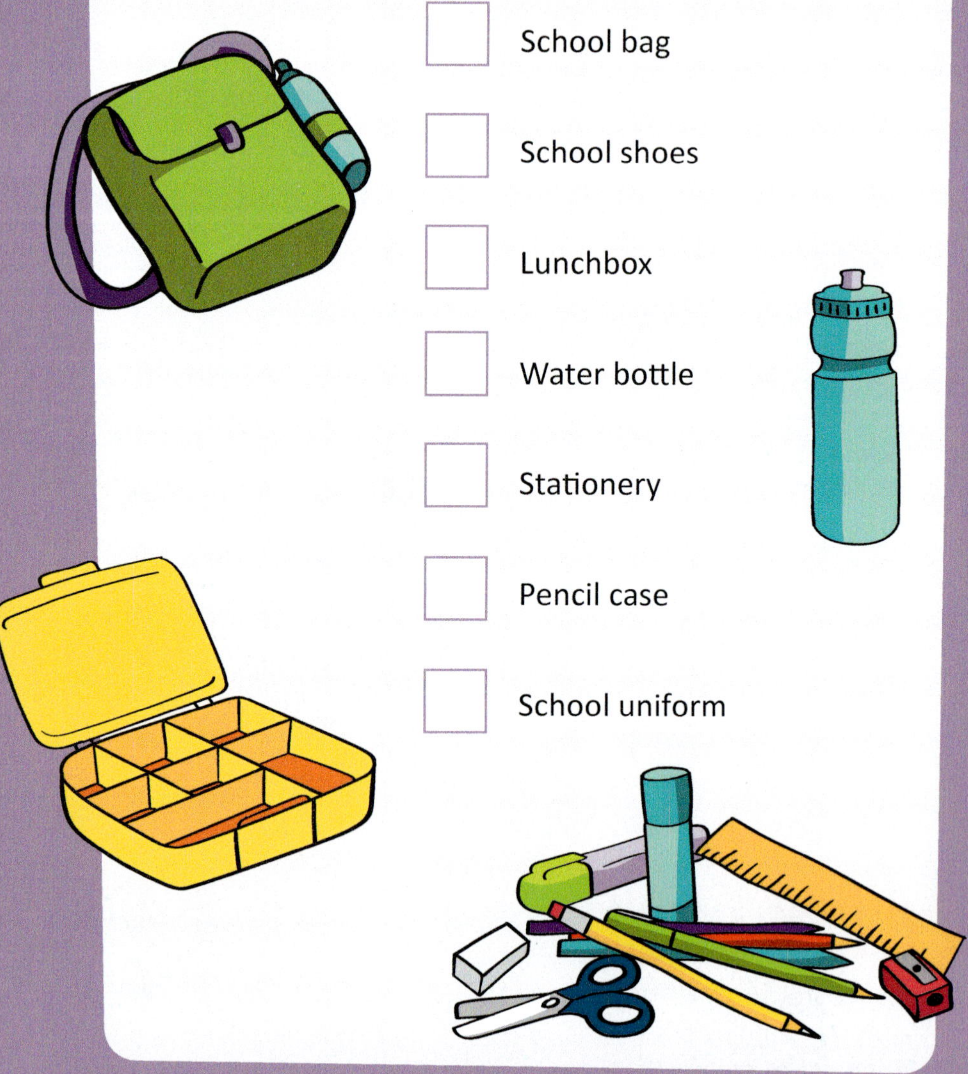

- [ ] School bag
- [ ] School shoes
- [ ] Lunchbox
- [ ] Water bottle
- [ ] Stationery
- [ ] Pencil case
- [ ] School uniform

Getting into a Routine

Morning routine

Attending school five days a week can be **VERY** tiring and can take a lot of energy. You might wake up feeling a bit tired and sleepy first thing in the morning, so the more you can prepare the night before, the better.

Getting organised for school is also called a **ROUTINE**. This means that you plan to do the **SAME** things at a similar time each day.

You can sit down with your parents or caregiver to plan what you need to do to prepare for the new school day.

For example:

- What time will you wake up each school morning?
- Will you pack your school bag the night before?
- Where will you set out your uniform?

It can be a helpful idea to write out a **CHECK LIST** of things you need to remember to do each morning in order of what needs to be done. You don't want to forget to pack your sports shoes, or even worse, your lunchbox!

Ben says...

In the mornings, I wake up and get dressed into my school uniform. I then eat my breakfast, which is usually cereal. Then I brush my teeth, make my bed and get my socks and shoes on. I put my lunchbox and drink bottle into my school bag and then I'm ready to go.

'Wake up early, like 7am. Get as much of your lunch and snacks as ready as you can, then you can watch some TV, get dressed and leave for school.'

Ben, aged 9

'My best advice for the morning is be quick! Otherwise you'll get in trouble.'

Isaac, aged 8 years

'Make sure you have your school clothes all ready at night so you don't have to find them in the morning.'

Judah, aged 10

'My best advice for getting ready for school in the morning is to wake up early! Prepare what you can the night before. Prioritise getting ready first, then you'll have time to play.'

Callum, aged 11

'My best tips for getting ready for school in the morning are: have everything ready the night before to save time in the morning! My schedule is to wake up to the alarm, have a wash or shower, get dressed, watch TV while eating breakfast. Then I pack my school bag, clean teeth, then out the door.'

Rocco, aged 11

A typical morning routine may look like this...

 7am wake up

 Wash my face

 Make my bed

 Eat breakfast

 Put on school uniform

 Put my lunch in school bag

 Put school books in school bag

 Brush teeth

 Brush hair

 Put my shoes on

 Leave for school

Write a list of what your morning school routine looks like...

What to pack in your school bag

- Lunch box
- Pencil case
- Water bottle
- Sun hat
- Reader and books
- Homework
- Sports clothes and shoes

What's in your school bag?

Write a list here of what you need to take to school.

Draw a picture of your school bag.

Things to leave at home

There are some items that I'm sure you would just love to bring to school with you. But there are some things that are far too precious or **NOT APPROPRIATE** to bring to school. These include any electronic devices. They should be left at home where they can be kept safe. Also, any items that are very important to you should be left at home.

Sometimes, you might want to bring in a special item especially for **SHOW & TELL**. That is okay, as long as you make a special arrangement with your parents. You could ask your teacher to put your special item away in a safe place at school until you need to get it out to show your classmates.

Keeping well

Eating well

School life is very busy, that's for sure. So, you will need to make sure that you take good care of your **HEALTH**. That includes making sure you eat well, drink lots of water, exercise and play, as well as getting a good night's sleep.

When we get the balance right, we should be feeling **GOOD!**

Sometimes, you might be feeling a little unwell, or catch a cold and might need some extra sleep. But if you look after yourself, hopefully you won't get sick too often.

One of the things that you may notice about school life is that it can be **VERY** tiring at times. You have to concentrate for periods of time, and are often very active. So, the **FIRST** thing you need to do each morning is make sure you eat a healthy breakfast! Your mind and body are much like a car, and need fuel to keep them going throughout the day.

Some healthy breakfast ideas:

- Toast with spreads (like Vegemite, jam or honey)
- Yoghurt
- Fruit (blueberries are **ESPECIALLY** good brain food!)
- Cereal
- Pancakes
- A smoothie

Eating well at school

You are going to be using your brain a lot during the school day. And your body needs to stay **HYDRATED** and be given lots of **ENERGY** to make it work at its best. This means you need to drink **WATER** and eat lots of **HEALTHY FOODS** throughout the day.

It's important that you include healthy foods in your lunch box that are good for your growing mind and body. Try and avoid taking sugary foods and junk foods like chips and sweet biscuits. (Save them for special occasions.)

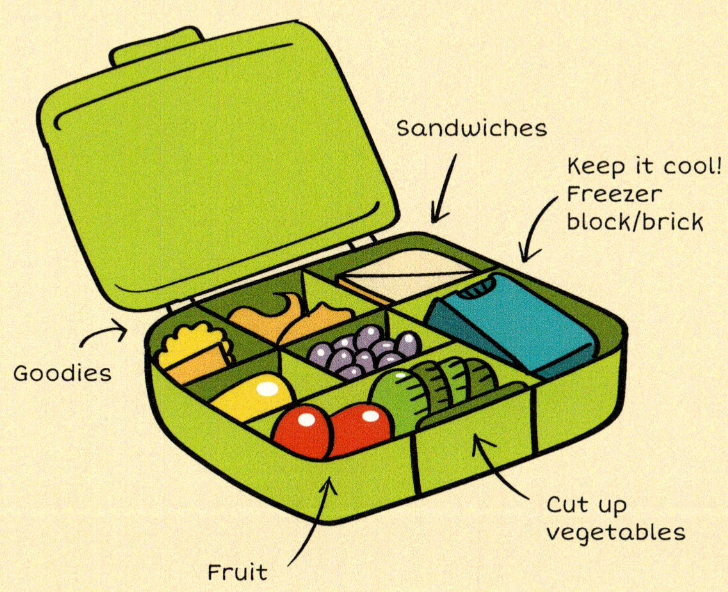

Things you could include in your school lunch box:

- Carrot, cucumber, celery sticks
- Cut-up fruits (different coloured fruits that are in-season)
- Your favourite dip
- Rice crackers
- Cheese sticks or cheese cut into cubes
- Falafels
- Sandwiches cut into small shapes
- Mini sausage and veggie rolls
- Pizza scrolls
- Mini cheese and Vegemite scrolls
- Mini muffins
- Zucchini slice
- Rolled up slices of ham or chicken loaf
- Cherry tomatoes
- Boiled egg

Ben says...

In my lunchbox I like to pack lots of fruit. Usually it's whatever is in season, like apples and pears, watermelon, and strawberries. In summer time I like peaches and mangoes. I enjoy snacking throughout the day at school and eat things like muesli bars, popcorn or rice crackers, and pretzels.

The food pyramid

The **FOOD PYRAMID** can help teach you about what foods you need to eat more of, and which ones to eat less often so you can keep a **HEALTHY BALANCE**.

The three groups of foods you eat from are often shown as a **FOOD PYRAMID**.

The top of the pyramid is the smallest part of the pyramid. It contains foods you should only eat sometimes.

The middle of the pyramid contains foods you should eat moderately (a medium amount). They are important for health, but we don't need too much of them.

The bottom of the pyramid is the biggest part. It contains the foods you should eat most of the time.

Based on Nutrition Australia information (www.nutritionaustralia.org)

Drink lots of water

Our bodies are made up of more than 70 per cent water.

We need to ensure we replace our fluids constantly (especially with the lots of running around that happens during the day at school.)

TWO LITRES (8 glasses of water) per day is recommended.

Fill a large water bottle with water at the beginning of the day before you go to school. Carry this around with you and drink from it as much as you can throughout the day. For extra flavour, you can add a couple of **STRAWBERRIES**, or a slice of **LEMON** or **LIME** or **ORANGES** or **MINT LEAVES**.

Sandwich or wrap filling ideas

Try some of these ideas and combinations:

- Honey
- Vegemite, with or without cheese
- Ham, with or without cheese
- Jam
- Shredded chicken with mayonnaise
- Egg and lettuce
- Avocado, with or without Vegemite
- Cheese, chicken and avocado
- Cheese and tomato
- Ham, cheese and tomato
- Salami, with or without cheese and lettuce
- Curried egg
- Falafels and lettuce
- Nutella
- Ham, cheese and avocado

School lunch recipes to try

Over the next few pages are a few recipes you could make with your parent or helpful adult for a tasty after school snack, or to add to your lunchbox.

Pizza scrolls

Time Allowance – 50 minutes

puff pastry
bacon, onion and cheese
tomato paste

What you'll need

- Frying pan
- Chopping board
- Baking trays x 2
- Wooden spoon
- Baking paper (so your scrolls don't stick to the tray)
- Sharp knife (An adult will help you chop up the bacon and onion)

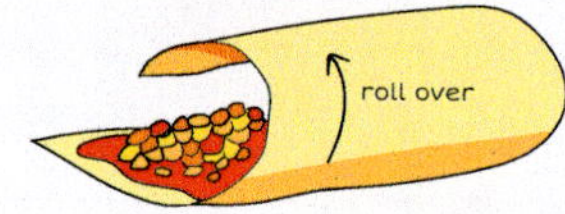

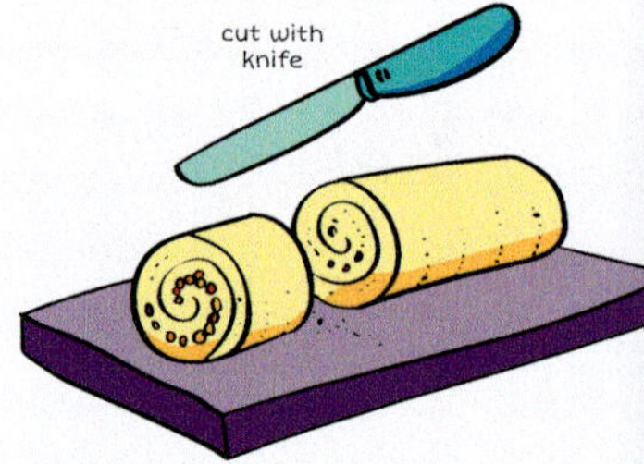

Ingredients

- 1 packet of frozen puff pastry slices (usually comes with 5 or 6 slices)
- 1 packet of rindless bacon (at least 5 slices)
- 1 onion (if you want to include onion)
- 1 small tub of tomato paste/pizza sauce
- 1 packet of grated cheese

NOTE: These yummy pizza scrolls can be frozen in freezer bags or containers to bring out the night before you pack your school lunch.

Method

1. Pre-heat the oven to 220 degrees (a helpful adult will be able to do this).
2. Separate and place puff pastry sheet on to the kitchen bench.
3. Chop bacon and onion into small pieces (you don't have to include onion if you really don't like the taste of it).
4. Place bacon and onion in a frying pan and cook until done.
5. Cover each piece of puff pastry sheet with a thin layer of tomato paste or pizza sauce.
6. Spread a layer of bacon and onion sparingly (this means not too much) over each puff pastry sheet.
7. Sprinkle grated cheese sparingly over each bacon mix.
8. Using an adult to help you, carefully roll one of the puff-pastry sheets from one end to the other (it will be quite full of ingredients) until it looks like a fat caterpillar. ☺
9. Place baking paper onto the baking pans or spray a light layer of baking oil directly onto the pan.
10. Place the caterpillar shaped filled pastry and gently (with help from an adult) slice through into thick sections – see illustrations.
11. Place each scroll carefully onto the baking tray, making sure you allow plenty of space around each scroll so that they don't get squashed together when they expand in the oven.
12. Bake in the oven for 10-15 minutes until the pastry looks cooked and the cheese has melted.

Savoury muffins

Time Allowance – 50 minutes

What you'll need

- Frying pan
- Chopping board
- Muffin trays x 2
- Wooden spoon
- Sharp knife (An adult will help you chop up the bacon and onion)
- Large mixing bowl

Ingredients

- 1 egg (beaten)
- 2 tablespoons of butter or margarine
- ½ onion
- ¾ cup of grated cheese
- 1 teaspoon of mixed herbs
- 2 tablespoons of chopped fresh parsley (optional)
- 1 packet of rindless bacon or fresh chopped ham
- 2 cups of self-raising flour
- ½ cup of milk
- A pinch of salt (optional)

Method

1. Pre-heat the oven to 200 degrees (ask a helpful adult to help with this.)
2. Grease (or spray lightly with cooking oil) muffin trays.
3. Mix together butter, egg, and milk in the mixing bowl, using the wooden spoon.
4. Add in sifted flour, a pinch of salt, herbs, parsley and grated cheese. Mix these together.
5. Chop bacon* and onion finely. (You will need an adult to help you with this.) Lightly fry these in a frying pan.
   *If not using bacon, you can finely chop some ham.
6. Mix onion and bacon/ham into the mixture in a bowl.
7. Place large tablespoons of mixture into each of the muffin tray spaces. (Make sure you only fill halfway with mixture, as it will rise in the oven as they cook.)
8. Sprinkle some extra grated cheese on top of the muffin mix.
9. Bake in the oven for 25-30 minutes.

NOTE:
These yummy savoury muffins can be frozen.

Ben's favourite banana & cinnamon muffins

Time allowance – 45 minutes

What you'll need:

- Muffin tray
- Wooden spoon
- Mixing bowl

Ingredients

- ½ cup of olive oil
- 1 cup of brown sugar
- 1 cup of Self Raising Flour
- 2 eggs
- ½ teaspoon of vanilla essence
- ½ teaspoon of cinnamon
- 4 very ripe bananas (the squishier the better)
- ½ cup of chopped nuts (such as almond flakes)
- Olive oil spray

*Sometimes, I add small pieces of my broken-up Easter Eggs that I haven't eaten. You can also add in half a cup of chopped chocolate pieces or choc chips.

Method

1. Mash up the bananas together in a bowl until they are really squishy.
2. Mix together in mixing bowl, oil, brown sugar, nuts, vanilla essence, cinnamon, eggs and mashed bananas.
3. Sift flour into the mixture.
4. Add in chocolate chips if you want to use them.
5. Spray the muffin tray lightly with olive oil.
6. Spoon all of the mixture evenly into each of the twelve muffin spaces.
7. Bake in a moderate oven for 20 minutes, or until cooked.
8. Once cooked, scoop each muffin out of the tray, taking care that they don't break apart. Allow to cool and then enjoy!

I always have to give at least half of my muffins to my Pa, and I always set aside one to go into my lunchbox the next day.

Make these in batches and you can freeze them use as needed.

Write out a favourite recipe here...

What are your favourite ideas to pack in your school lunchbox? Draw them in the spaces below.

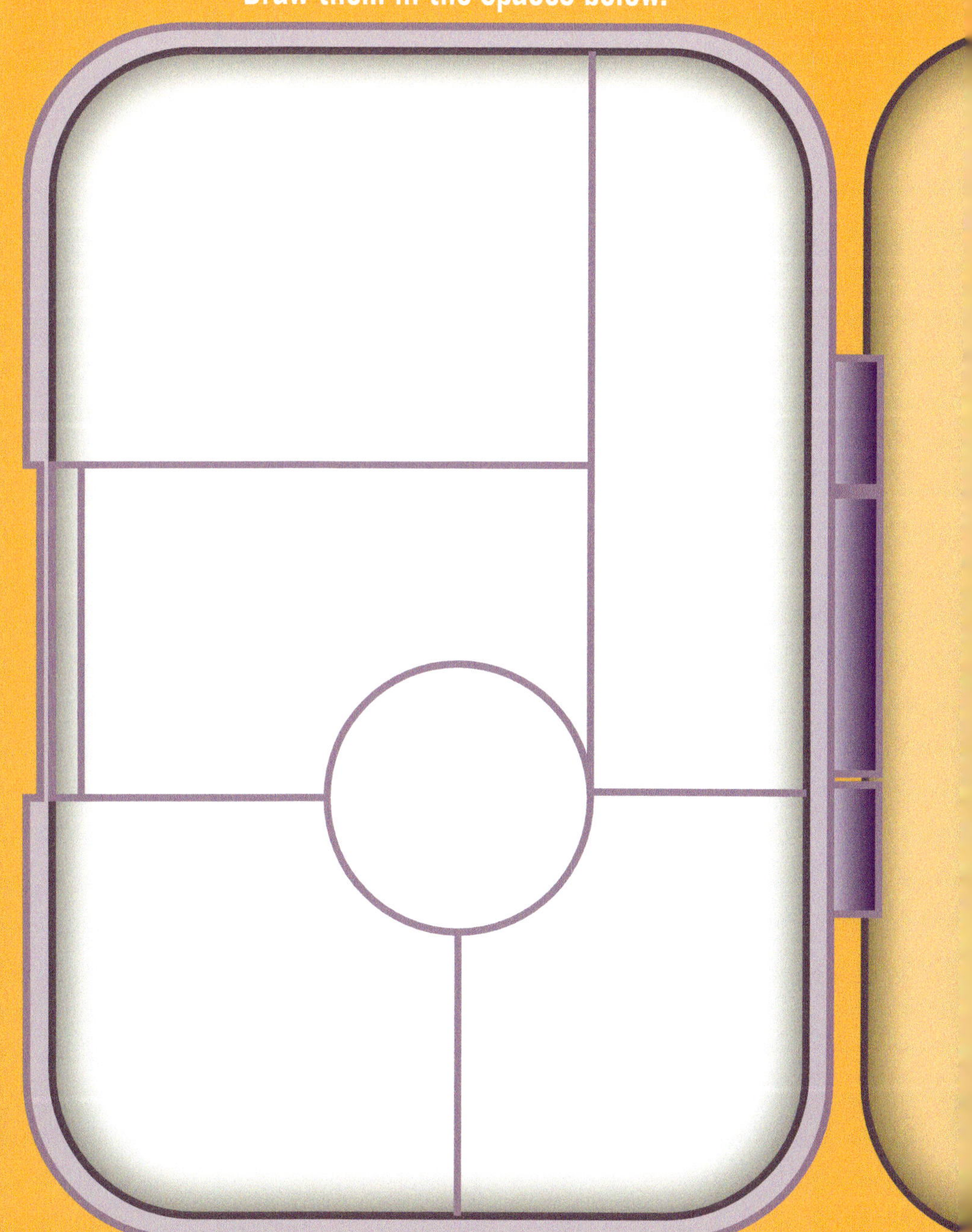

Sleep

When you are in school, you need **MORE SLEEP** than ever because you are having to focus much more during the day. You are also probably being a lot more active at school as well.

Did you know that when you sleep, your body is working hard to **RESTORE** and **REBUILD** important cells that help to fight off germs and illness? Your body needs to **REBOOT** – much like a computer. So, you need to give it rest time.

Sleep also gives your brain the opportunity to sort through important and valuable information from your day, and file it away for later. Your brain never stops working!

How much sleep do I need?

When you were first born, you probably slept a lot more than you do now. You also would have had a couple of sleeps during the day. Because you are now at school, you need to have between ten and twelve hours of sleep every night. Of course, this might vary depending on how your day went, or how busy your week is. For example, sometimes you might have a special family event during the school week and you go to bed a little later one night. That may just mean that you need to catch up on a little more sleep the next night, or on the weekend.

Try and aim for at **LEAST** ten hours of sleep each school night to allow your mind and body to function at their best during the school day.

What you can do if you are having trouble sleeping

It can be **VERY** frustrating if you are in bed and trying to fall asleep, and you just **CANNOT!** Here are some helpful tips that might help you have a better night's sleep.

SLEEP TIPS

- Listen to some calming music
- Turn off electronics
- Have a warm bath or shower before going to bed
- Read a book for 20 minutes before bed
- Make sure your room is not too **WARM** or **COLD**
- Write in a diary for ten minutes about your day
- Have a warm drink
- Pray (or have a parent pray with you)
- Try some breathing exercises

Ben says...

My bedtime is 8pm at night, so I usually begin getting ready for bed about thirty minutes before then. I get my pyjamas on, brush my teeth, and I might have a little drink of water. Then I hop into my bed, with my bedside lamp on. I do deep breathing exercises where I take 5 deep breaths in, and 5 deep breaths out. This relaxes my brain and I usually fall asleep straight away.

'When I am having trouble falling asleep, I sing to myself.'

Ethan, aged 9

'My advice is to relax your face and close your eyes.'

Jo, aged 9

'My suggestion is lie on your bed for about five minutes in the dark and close your eyes.'

Athan, aged 8

'My advice is to read a book or draw a mind map of all the random things in your head. Then it should be easier to go to sleep. Or if you have a prism light, you can watch it make patterns on your roof.'

Ethan, aged 12

'I sit in my bed and read for about fifteen minutes. This makes me feel sleepy.'

Christopher, aged 9

'I have a sleep routine at night. I go to the bathroom, brush my teeth, have a drink of water, then I lie in my bed with the lamp on for about ten minutes before my mum comes in and prays with me. Then I usually fall asleep.'

Sebastian, aged 10

It's important to make sure that you get a good amount of exercise every day. When we are **ACTIVE** and get outside, we release the extra energy we have built up, as well as the endorphins in our brain that make us feel happy.

Perhaps you are involved in a local sporting team or club. Or you may just enjoy being outside, running around and exercising with your siblings or friends.

Things you might do to stay active

- Basketball
- Football
- Skipping
- Tree climbing
- Calisthenics
- Rollerskating
- Skateboarding
- Building cubby houses
- Cheerleading
- Cricket
- Soccer
- Athletics
- Gymnastics
- Bike riding

Sometimes we can get caught up watching television, spending time online, or playing video games. These activities can be fun, but they can prevent us from getting our bodies moving. So, make sure you build at least **20 MINUTES** of exercise into your daily routine and get moving!

You can dress up, play make-believe and pretend you are anyone or anywhere.

What do you like to do for exercise?

Draw a picture of your favourite activity to help you stay active.

Making Friends at School

Making friends

I actually met my very first school friend when she moved in next door to me. Pretty much from the first time we met we became the best of friends. It helped that we lived next door to each other too, so we could often play together after school.

We started school together in Prep (Reception).

I still remember that our teacher was Mrs Bowler. She was tall, friendly and always smiling. There were about nineteen other students in our class. Our school was very small. It was in a small country town, but we **LOVED** it!

The one thing I recall is that our teacher actually helped us to make friends within the classroom. She would often encourage us to sit next to someone different for some activities, or to play with larger groups of friends during play time. This was great advice for me and my friend too, because it meant that we got to know **OTHER FRIENDS** as well.

Soon after we started school, they built a brand-new school closer to our home, so many of us moved to the new school. There we had the opportunity to get to know many more friends, as the school was much bigger.

At recess and lunch, we would play games where we would do lots of **PRETENDING**. We would imagine we were from another time, like the olden days, and sometimes we pretended we were in the middle of a large game where there were 'goodies' and 'baddies.' We had so much fun that we often felt disappointed when we heard the bell going to come back inside for class.

The main thing I remember throughout my primary school years is that we made sure we **INCLUDED** lots of different people in our games. It would have been easy for myself and my best friend to just play by ourselves, but we would have missed out on making so many other friends.

And I **STILL** see some of those friends I made in primary school **MANY** years later. We say hello and smile at each other and remember how much we enjoyed our school years together.

Ben says...

If you are out at recess by yourself, try and find one or more of your friends to play with. Otherwise, find a teacher out on yard duty who is wearing a bright vest, and let them know that you are lost, or need help finding someone to play with.

Try not to worry. There will be people at school to show you around. If you need any help, ask any people in your class, including your teacher. And be friendly.

'If you're worried about making new friends, try to talk with kids in your class who seem similar to you. Try not to worry about it too much because there would be other kids who are feeling the same as you. Remember, you are not alone!'

Rocco, aged 11

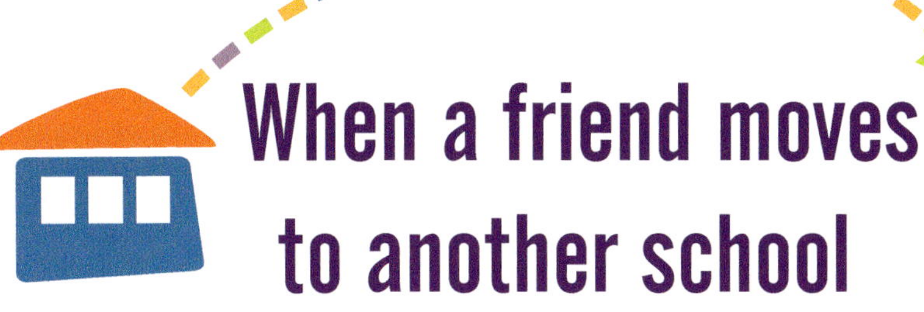

When a friend moves to another school

Sometimes, for many reasons, a friend may have to move to another school.

Perhaps they move away from where they live or for other reasons that you might not understand for now.

This might make you feel a bit **SAD**, or you might worry that you will **MISS** them terribly. But it doesn't mean you may not see them anymore. Your friend may still live close by, so you can have visits on weekends or over the holidays. If they move away, you can write letters and cards to your friend to keep in regular contact.

Try to remember, just because you may not see your friend at school every day doesn't mean you can't still be friends. You can still stay in touch. Think about some interesting ways you can still connect.

Making new friends

One of my closest friendships came from someone I met at the school I teach. From an early point of meeting, we've just made each other laugh, and laugh! It's always felt like the chats and laughs have come so easy. Above all, we totally RESPECT each other. That means, even if we disagree about something the other says, we stay friends.

Other friends I have formed over the years have come from living in the same street! Almost every day, you'll see a neighbour and say 'Hi'. The more we TALK, the more we form friendships.

I've made many other friends along the way just simply by being INTERESTED in others, smiling when I meet someone new and ASKING QUESTIONS to get to know them better.

It doesn't take much to say hello to someone you haven't met before, but I am sure glad I have done this on many occasions. If I hadn't tried talking with people, I would have missed out on some pretty awesome friendships!

You will have the opportunity to meet many new friends while you are at school. Some of the friends you make might even move on with you later to high school (but that's a bit later down the track when you are much older ☺.)

How do you make new friends?

One of my favourite quotes says:

'THE ONLY WAY TO HAVE A FRIEND, IS TO BE ONE!'
RALPH WALDO EMERSON

What this means is, if you want to make new friends, you have to practice **BEING** a friend to others.

The best way to make friends... is to be friendly!

You need to give others an opportunity to get to know you.

I know that this can feel a bit scary for some people at first, but try to remember that just about everyone else is feeling just as **NERVOUS** and perhaps **WORRIED** about making new friends as you are. ☺

Tips for making new friends at school

'You can make more friends in two months by becoming really interested in other people, than you can in two years by trying to get other people interested in you.'

Dale Carnegie

Sometimes, it's difficult to know how to begin a conversation with someone you don't know very well, or at all. There are some things you can do to let someone know that you would like the opportunity to talk with them...

Be interested

Try and begin a conversation with someone new by showing that you are interested in **THEM** first. If they are new to your school, you might begin by asking them what school they came from, what they like to do for fun, or how many family members they have. Once you begin asking questions, you are sure to find something in common to talk about fairly quickly.

Use eye contact

This probably seems like something **SO SIMPLE** but it's something that many boys forget! Even before you first go up to someone and begin a conversation, use eye contact. Look them in the eyes and make sure you nod, smile and look at them when you are talking. When you look someone in the eyes, you know that they have seen you. This is a good thing to do as it lets the other person know that YOU are interested in talking to THEM!

Smile

When we smile, our entire face lights up. A simple smile says SO MUCH! It says that you are willing to make a new friend. It says that you are happy to talk with the other person. It says that you are interested in getting to know them and that they are VALUED! Most importantly, a smile costs you ABSOLUTELY NOTHING! Come to think of it, you have a never-ending supply of smiles available, so make sure you use them often!

Use a soft, kind voice

When introducing yourself to a new friend, it's a good idea to NOT use your outside yelling voice or loud tone. Use a gentle, kind voice so that the other person can hear you properly and understand what you are saying.

Ask questions!

When you are first getting to know a new friend (or haven't seen them in a while), make sure you ask lots of questions to find things out about the other person. Sure, it's great to share your own stories and interests, but make sure you also ask questions to get to know the other person. (Have a look at the next page for some ideas.)

Be yourself

The best advice you could ever follow is to **BE YOURSELF!** No one else can be you, and you bring something to your friendship groups that no one else does.

Sometimes, there is very real pressure on us to try and act like someone else. We can think that our personality is boring and uninteresting. But that's not being real. The problem with not being yourself when you first make a new friend is that you have to keep up appearances. That means, if you pretend that you really like rock climbing, pretty soon, your friend will want to go rock climbing with you because it's something that you said you enjoy. Or maybe you say you love watching a specific television show. Before you know it, your new friend has just invited you over after school this week to watch it. And you were just trying to sound impressive!

JUST STOP! The real you is fine and wonderful, and worth getting to know (even if your hobby is collecting rocks!).

'Find me, or someone who is kind, and I will make friends with them, because kind people do that.'

Ben, aged 9

'Try not to worry about making friends – you will get them whether you like it or not. It will happen.'

Micah, aged 12

'Try not to be too worried because you will always find someone who wants to be your friend.'

Judah, aged 10

'If you don't have anyone to play with at recess or lunch, I would suggest going to the library, as there are probably other kids who don't have anyone to play with. Also, talk more to the other kids in your class when you can. Try to expand your friendship group.'

Rocco, aged 11

'Try to look for other children who have the same interests as you. Speak to them and hopefully you will become friends.'

Judah, aged 10

'If you're worried about making new friends, try to talk with kids in your class who seem similar to you. Try not to worry about it too much because there would be other kids who are feeling the same as you. Remember, you are not alone!'

Rocco, aged 11

Making new friends

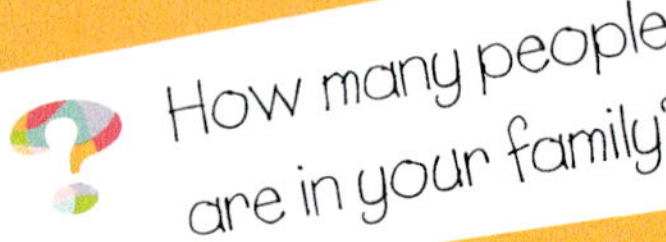

How many people are in your family?

What is the strangest/funniest pet you've owned?

If you could be an animal, which one would you choose and why?

Have you ever met anyone famous?

How many schools have you been to?

Have you ever travelled overseas?

What was your most embarrassing moment?

What is your favourite colour?

Do you play a musical instrument?

If you could have an entire day to do anything you wanted, what would you do?

What is the weirdest gift you've ever received?

Have you ever been to the circus, and where was it?

What is your all-time favourite movie?

What are you most scared of – mice or spiders?

at school...

Questions you can ask a new friend at school

What is your favourite television show?

If you could choose a superpower, what would you choose and why?

Who do you admire most and why?

Do you have a favourite sporting team that you follow?

Is there a pet you wish you could own but your parents won't let you?

What was your favourite birthday you have had, and what made it so special?

Do you have any strange habits?

What would you change about yourself and why?

What special talents do you have?

What is your favourite thing to do on a rainy day?

What do you want to do when you grow up?

Interview some new friends in you

Name

Age Grade

Family members

Pets names (if they have any)

Favourite movie

3 activities they like to do for fun

Draw a picture of them

Name

Age Grade

Family members

Pets names (if they have any)

Favourite movie

3 activities they like to do for fun

Draw a picture of them

class

Name

Age Grade

Family members

Pets names (if they have any)

Favourite movie

3 activities they like to do for fun

Draw a picture of them

Name

Age Grade

Family members

Pets names (if they have any)

Favourite movie

3 activities they like to do for fun

Draw a picture of them

What you can do if you are feeling shy

If you feel a bit SHY around others, or find it difficult to go up to a new person and say hello, try not to worry about it. Some students may feel more confident than others when they are at school.

Some boys have no problem at all when they are at home with their family where they feel COMFORTABLE and safe to be themselves, but feel shy and worried when they get to school. Please don't worry if this sounds like you. Everyone is different. Do you know that even some teachers feel SHY around other teachers and friends? Even famous people you see on TV can feel shy about meeting new people, but can feel perfectly okay when they have to be on camera.

Some ideas to help if you are feeling shy at school:

- Take some big, deep breaths
- Relax
- Smile (this also helps you to relax)
- Choose one person at a time to sit with or play with at recess
- Let your teacher know how you are feeling, and they might be able to help introduce you to a new friend.

What do you like to do at recess and lunchtime?

'I like to play soccer with my friends at recess.'

Ethan, aged 10

'At recess I enjoy playing tag.'

Sam, aged 8

'At recess I enjoy chatting with my friends and playing 'down ball.''

Judah, aged 10

'At recess and lunch I like to use my imagination to play activities – like from a TV show, you can imagine you are a part of the show.'

Alex, aged 8

'My favourite thing to do at recess are drawing, playing tiggy, cops and robbers, and reading is always good.'

Callum, aged 11

'At recess we like to play tiggy and talk about stuff that we find cool.'

Leo, aged 11

'At recess and lunch time I like to eat and talk with friends. I like to play handball sometimes but mainly quiet sit-down games like mafia and spy.'

Rocco, aged 11

'I like to play with my friends during break times. We usually walk around the school, and sometimes we play running races where we set a course and time how long it takes for each of us to complete it. It's often a race to see who can complete the course the quickest.'

Ben, aged 9

Learning tolerance

As friends, we all need to learn **TOLERANCE**, because sometimes we will be friends with others who do frustrate us by the way they behave. It can easily get us down. We all need to learn to tolerate others and their personalities. You can't always control who you will spend time with – whether that be friends on your netball or basketball team, or relatives at a big family barbeque. Sometimes, you need to **SMILE** and remember to be interested in what others have to say.

As a side note, being tolerant **DOESN'T** mean you have to put up with behaviour that is unacceptable, such as bullying, gossiping or physical threats. This is **NEVER** okay. But just remember that one day you will be out in the big wide world working in a job, and you can't control the different personalities you will work with.

Learning to get along with others and accept that we are created differently is a part of growing up.

You cannot control others' behaviours, but you can always control **YOUR OWN!**

Bullying

Dealing with bullies

For whatever reason, some people find it necessary to treat others with unkindness. Mostly, when someone chooses to be unkind or **BULLY** another person, it says a lot more about them than it does about the person actually being targeted.

Often, someone who threatens, teases, is nasty to others or tries to make others **FEEL SMALL**, is struggling with their own thoughts of being sad, alone, unloved or having a poor self-image. If they make others feel small and inadequate, perhaps they will feel bigger and more important.

But bullying others doesn't work that way. The bully ends up looking unkind, small and just plain nasty.

Bullying hurts!

It may not necessarily be physical bullying that you are experiencing, but **EMOTIONAL** bullying (being teased, talked about or deliberately left out of games or conversations) can hurt just as much!

What Bullying is NOT!

Bullying is not just saying something nasty to someone else – for example: 'Your hair is really ugly!' or 'You're no fun!'

That is simply being nasty. It is not okay, that's for sure, but it's not bullying. Bullying can be targeted at one person and can be **REPEATED!** It may be when someone is continually singling you out and deliberately making you feel small.

What is Bullying?

Bullying can include...

- Hurting someone **PHYSICALLY** (hitting, pulling hair)
- **NAME-CALLING**
- Deliberately **EXCLUDING** someone (leaving them out)
- **GOSSIPING** (talking behind someone's back or making up stories that are untrue)

Usually, these behaviours become bullying when it happens **CONSISTENTLY** (often or all of the time). It can feel like it is never going to stop, and it can leave you feeling angry, sad, alone, confused, scared or distressed.

Tell someone who cares about you!

Here are some things you can do if another kid (or older person) is often causing you to feel small and sad.

Tell an adult

Even if the person bullying you tells you not to tell anyone, you **MUST** let a person know (an adult you trust, such as your teacher or parent) about what is happening to you.

No one deserves to feel scared, intimidated or small because of how someone else is behaving.

Say 'No!'

As soon as you say this single, powerful word – '**NO!**' – you are letting bullies know – loud and clear – that what they are doing or saying is not okay. If you struggle a bit with this at first, start by saying it under your breath or in your mind until you soon have the courage to say it out loud, with authority. You are worth it! Saying 'No' also lets everyone else around you know that what is happening is not okay. They become witnesses to the bullying and your desire for it to stop.

Stand tall and have confidence

Bullies are looking for people they can steal from. They want your confidence. And they only gain it by taking yours. Try to remember that bullies are really just people who lack confidence in themselves. Bullies try to make others feel inferior to hide their own insecurities. When you remember this fact, you realise that bullies are just people who lack confidence.

Don't look the other way if you see someone being bullied

If you see friends or others being bullied, you owe it to them to let someone know. Tell a teacher or your parents what is happening.

Remember that if a person is hurting you, they are likely hurting others as well.

Need a bit more information or help?
Take a look at this great website:

bullyingnoway.gov.au

Write about a time when someone was unkind to you. How did you respond?

Getting to know your teacher

Getting to know your teacher

When you begin school, you will have a class teacher. They will spend a lot of time with you each day. Teachers are wonderful people. (I should know because I am one. ☺)

Their job is to help you feel **COMFORTABLE** and **HAPPY** at school, and to assist you in solving any problems you might experience.

Your teacher will also teach you many new and exciting things like:

- **MATHS** (learning and counting numbers, and adding them together, for example)
- **WORDS** (learning what they mean and how to pronounce them)
- 

And you'll have many opportunities in class to create, paint, draw, explore, investigate and learn about so many amazing things.

Remember, it will take **SOME TIME** for you to get to know your teacher, just as they get to know you.

Make sure you talk to your teacher if you are feeling WORRIED, UNSURE, UNWELL, or even if you have just forgotten where something is.

You can also SHARE many good and exciting things with your teacher, such as what you did on the weekend, if you got a new pet, or even if you have a new baby brother or sister.

What do you love most about your teachers?

I really like my teacher. He is funny and does crazy things like, at the door when we come in from a break, he will squirt hand sanitizer onto our hands, and then he does the same to himself but he makes funny actions with his hands when he does it. This makes us laugh. He also has a timer that he puts on during class. When the timer goes off, our teacher will sing a funny song like 'Twinkle, twinkle little star.' He's a great teacher. ☺

Ben, aged 9

'My teacher is so kind and she always stays with people who need her help. If you need her to help you with anything, she will just answer it and be kind to you. If anything goes wrong, you can always depend on her help.'

Hunter, aged 10

'I love it that my teacher has a good sense of humour and is funny. I like it when teachers are strict, but still fair, and when they are not too serious, but still get the point across about the learning.'

Rocco, aged 11

'I love that my teacher is kind.'

Asher, aged 7

What I like most about my teacher she is kind.'

Ethan, ages 10

'My teacher Mrs. Williams is really funny because she makes the work fun and plays lots of games after maths.'

Oscar, aged 9

'My favourite thing about my teacher is that if I make a mistake, she helps me.'

Alex, aged 8

'I love my teacher because she is so kind.'

Jarrah, aged 8.

'What I love most about my teacher is that she is kind.'

Sam, aged 8.

'I had two class teachers for grade 5, and I loved getting to know them both. I appreciate their patience and help with the work I had trouble with.'

Callum, aged 11

'The best thing about my teacher is that she is friendly and willing to make allowances to support students.'

Micah, aged 12

'The thing I love most about my teacher is that she is funny and lets us get away with stuff.'

Isaac, aged 8

'The best thing about my teachers is that they are funny and caring.'

Judah, aged 10

'My teacher is kind and she is funny.'

Ben, aged 9

'What I love most about my teacher is that she loves her job, and is caring and helpful.'

Jackson, aged 9

Interview your teacher

You might like to ask your teacher if you can interview them. (Pretend you are a reporter for a newspaper. ☺)

My teacher's name

What is your favourite food?

Have you ever broken a bone before? Where?

What is your favourite holiday destination?

Do you have pets at home? What are their names?

What sports team do you follow?

What do you like to do to relax?

What is the BEST thing about being a teacher?

What is the WORST thing about being a teacher?

Do you have children?

What is your least favourite food?

What is your favourite colour?

What month is your birthday?

What is the best gift you have ever received?

Have you travelled to other countries? Where?

How long have you worked at this school for?

What is your favourite music to listen to?

If you weren't a teacher, what do you think you'd be doing?

School
Days

A typical school day

No day is ever going to be exactly the same at school, but there will certainly be some ROUTINE and STRUCTURE to your days that will help you feel more settled at school.

Firstly, when you arrive at school each day, you will HANG YOUR SCHOOL BAG on the hook provided and bring your BOOKS and PENCIL CASE into your classroom, if they are not already in there. You may also have your READER or other books to return to the classroom.

Your class teacher might begin each school day by having you sit on the floor in front of them, or you may sit at your desk.

The first thing your teacher needs to do is MARK YOUR ATTENDANCE at school (often called marking the roll), because they need to know who is at school on each particular day, and if someone is away ill.

If you are running late to school, which can sometimes happen for a variety of reasons, make sure you check in at the school office or reception so that they can SIGN YOU IN. That way, everyone knows you are safely at school.

Your teacher might begin your morning by telling you what to expect throughout the day, what lessons you'll be having, and any special events that are happening. They might remind you of a notice that needs to be returned, or homework. Perhaps it is someone's birthday and they are to be celebrated that day. Your teacher might even sing a song, or even pray with your class.

Different teachers will have many different ways of beginning the day. They will make sure you feel **WELCOMED**, **RELAXED**, and **SETTLED** for the new day ahead.

Different subjects at school

During the school day, you may do many activities that will grow your mind and teach you new skills.

These will include:

Reading

Writing

Spelling

Maths (learning about numbers and fractions, addition and multiplication)

Sport / physical education

History (famous people and what they did – such as explorers, inventors and writers)

Geography (countries, cities, landmarks)

Science – how life and the universe works (gravity, animals and insects, volcanoes)

Art (drawing, painting, building, papier mâché)

Music

Homework pouch

Often, children are given a **HOMEWORK POUCH** or **FOLDER** at school which is used to transport your homework, take home readers, school diary, and notices to and from home.

This will be labelled with your name and will be a very important part of being an organised student.

Homework pouch

A word on tests

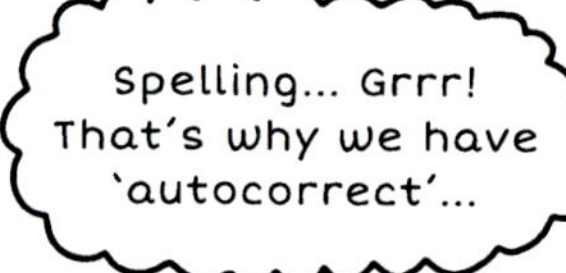

Throughout your years in primary school, there will be times when you will have tests on many areas of your learning. Some children become very NERVOUS and WORRIED about tests.

PLEASE DO NOT WORRY!

You will have lots of experiences of tests in school, over many years, and they are simply ONE WAY in which teachers can measure where you are at with a whole range of topics and subjects. Teachers are required to gather important information to HELP YOU with your learning. Often, they are able to make adjustments or give you extra assistance in an area of learning by assessing you with your work.

Remember, tests can only give information to your teacher about what you recall on that day at that time. They don't reveal SO many other things you are amazing at, such as being a good friend to others, a helpful student in the classroom, an incredible artist, or a great sport.

School/Classroom Rules

A part of being a member of any community involves following RULES or GUIDELINES that are created to keep everyone safe and well.

At school, all students need to feel SAFE and able to learn at their best.

Your class teacher may begin the school year by discussing some class guidelines with you. They may even ask your class to be involved in creating a set of class rules.

These may include:

- Raising your hand when you want to speak in class
- Taking it in turns
- Washing your hands before and after lessons
- Following the teacher's instructions
- Taking care of school property
- Being kind to one another
- Not going out of bounds in the playground

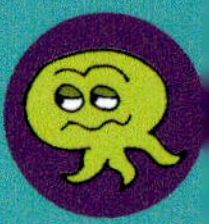

Write some school rules you think would be important to follow...

Before and after school care

Many parents have to work at different hours that may not suit school hours for pick up and drop off. So, some schools offer before and after school care.

You may arrive at school EARLIER than many other students and attend before school care. You may even enjoy breakfast with some other students. Or, you may attend AFTER school care until your parent or caregiver are able to pick you up.

These are run by FRIENDLY and RESPONSIBLE adults. They will often have activities for you to do whilst you attend.

Show and tell

When I was in primary school, I always got excited when it was my day to do **SHOW AND TELL**. Time is set aside for students to bring in something special from home to share with their classmates. Sometimes, you might even be able to arrange to have a small pet brought in with your parent or caregiver – just for a short time, as part of your show and tell.

If it is something very valuable, you are best to leave it at home, because unfortunately, accidents can happen at school and items can be broken or lost. If you **REALLY** want to bring in a valuable item, ask your parents, or another caregiver to bring it in for show and tell, and then take it back home.

Show and tell can be a wonderful opportunity to allow others in your class to get to know you better.

Show and tell ideas

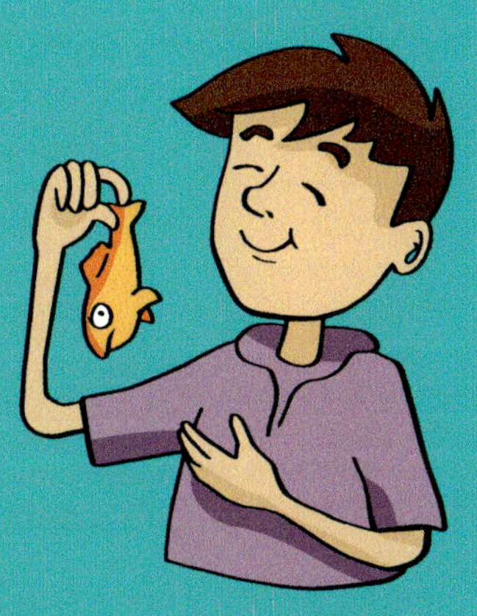

- Favourite photos
- An award you received
- A special ornament
- Favourite books
- Sports equipment
- A small pet (maybe not your goldfish!)
- A special collection
- Special photos in frames
- Art or paintings
- A holiday album
- Special toys
- Things you've built with Lego
- Your new baby brother or sister
- Favourite dress ups

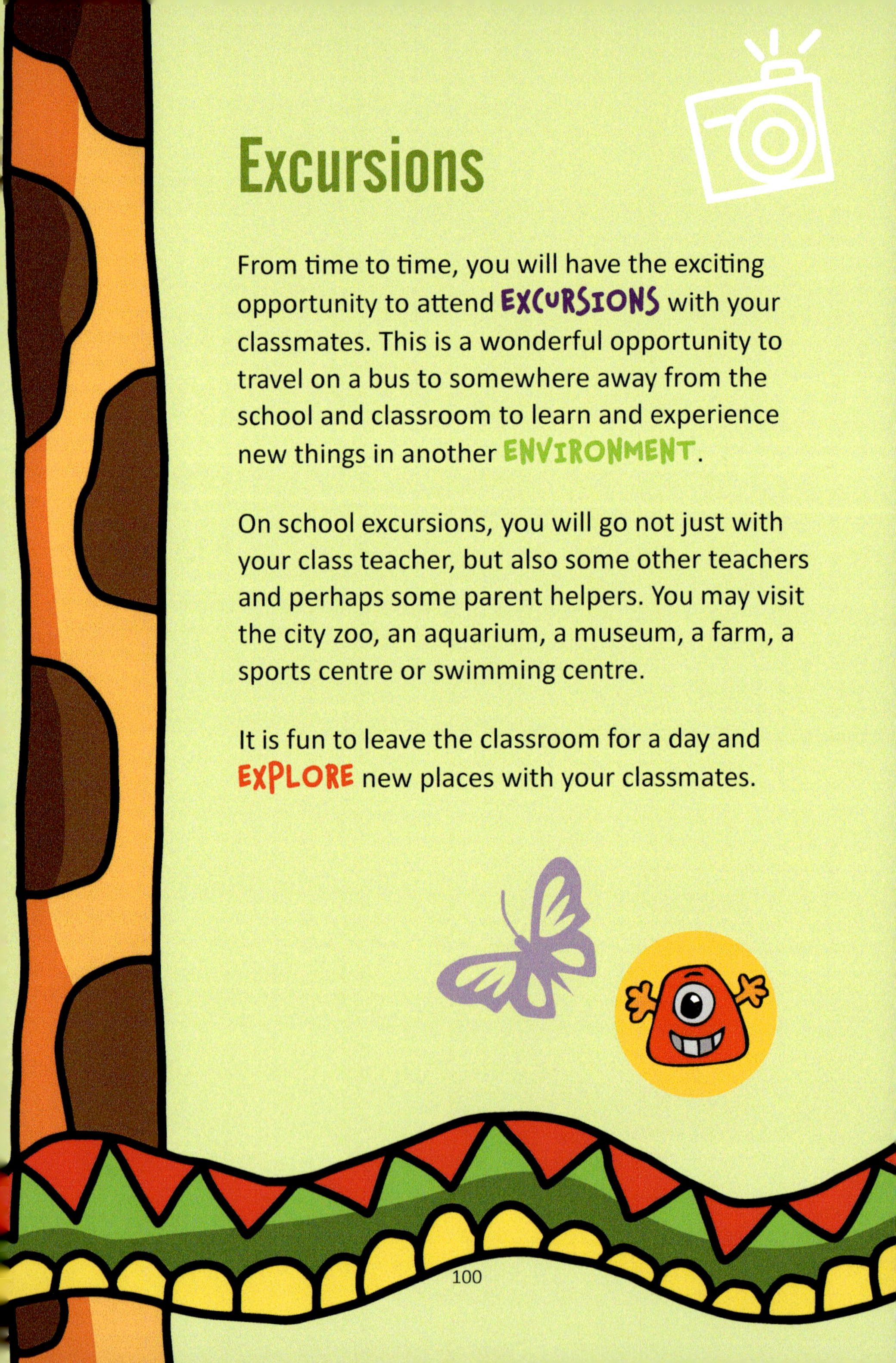

Excursions

From time to time, you will have the exciting opportunity to attend **EXCURSIONS** with your classmates. This is a wonderful opportunity to travel on a bus to somewhere away from the school and classroom to learn and experience new things in another **ENVIRONMENT**.

On school excursions, you will go not just with your class teacher, but also some other teachers and perhaps some parent helpers. You may visit the city zoo, an aquarium, a museum, a farm, a sports centre or swimming centre.

It is fun to leave the classroom for a day and **EXPLORE** new places with your classmates.

Write a story about your favourite excursion or special visitor to school...

School camps and sleepovers

There may be opportunities during your primary school years to go on a SCHOOL CAMP. Sometimes you might start with an overnight sleepover at school, and then go on a proper camp with your teacher and other adult helpers when you are a bit older.

School camps can be loads of FUN; however, for some children, the thought of being away from home and their family for even one night can be a little SCARY, or make them feel ANXIOUS or WORRIED.

It is perfectly okay if you feel a bit worried about being away from home. Many children (and even adults!) would prefer to be at home where they feel SAFE and SECURE. However, school camp can be lots of FUN, full of new adventures, new places to see and things to experience. You also have the opportunity to have a sleepover with some of your friends from class.

Your teachers will make sure that you have everything you need to ensure that you have a fun experience on camp. They will send home a notice to your parents or caregiver so that they know exactly where you are going, for how long (usually one or two sleeps) and what to bring.

If you are concerned at all about going on school camp, make sure you talk to an adult about how you are feeling. It might be helpful to take along your favourite teddy or a photo with you – something that reminds you of home.

What to bring on camp or school sleepover

- Your pillow
- Sleeping bag or other bedding (some camps provide these)
- Your favourite teddy bear or photo from home
- Bath towel
- Hair brush
- Toothbrush and toothpaste
- Small bottle of shampoo and conditioner
- Soap
- A warm waterproof jacket (for winter)
- Bathers and towel (if you are swimming)
- A few changes of clothes – tracksuit pants and jumpers
- Underwear and socks – several pairs
- A change of shoes
- A small day pack with snacks, lunch and water bottle

Leave electronic devices at home. You don't need these on school camp. Your teachers will always have a phone and can call your parents or caregiver if you need them.

What if I feel sick while I'm on camp?

If you **FEEL SICK** while you are away from home, make sure you tell your teacher, parent helper or any other adult. Make sure you tell them exactly what is wrong. Sometimes you might just feel funny in your stomach because you are **NERVOUS** or **WORRIED** about being away from home. That's perfectly okay too. ☺

Sometimes, just talking about how you are feeling can help settle those pesky butterflies in your tummy.

If at **ANY** time you are feeling unwell – even if it's in the middle of the night – it is okay to get up and tell the teacher or adult that is taking care of you. That's exactly what they are there for.

Other things you can do

- Take a few deep breaths
- Try and relax
- Tell an adult how you are feeling (they will know best how to help you)
- Think about how you'll soon be back home again with lots of **NEW MEMORIES** about your **ADVENTURES** on school camp.
- Pray

Handling wobbly days

Every single person occasionally has a **WOBBLY DAY** (even teachers do!)

Many things can cause a wobbly day. For example, perhaps you didn't get a good night's sleep. Maybe you left an important book at home that you wanted to bring to school. You may have been feeling a bit unwell, or fussy, or unsocial. Maybe, you found it **REALLY** difficult to concentrate in class today, or perhaps you were having some problems with friends.

Everyone, no matter who they are – can have **WOBBLY** days. These are days when it seems that nothing is going right. You may notice adults have them sometimes.

If you are at school, and you **KNOW** you are having a wobbly day – it's okay to tell your teacher.

The things to remember is this:

TODAY WAS JUST A WOBBLY DAY.

And when you lay your head on your pillow tonight, you will fall asleep and you get a brand-new day to begin again tomorrow.

And you can expect that tomorrow will be just **FINE**.

What can you do on a wobbly day?

When I have a wobbly day, I make sure I do at least **ONE THING** that I enjoy doing. It might be having a warm bath, writing in my diary, or watching my favourite movie or television program. Or I might go on a walk with my dog. Often, I just make sure I go to bed early so that my mind and body have a **GOOD REST**.

Write some things you could do if you have had a wobbly day?

Can you recall a time that you had a wobbly day?

What did you do to make yourself feel better?

Homework

Why do we have homework?

When you are in the first few years of primary school, you may have small amounts of **HOMEWORK** to take home to complete.

Homework is given for a few reasons:

- to help you practice your **READING**
- to help you learn your **SPELLING** words
- to practise **MATH** problems
- to **FINISH OFF** a task not completed at school.

Mostly, homework is set in primary school to help you to practise things you learn during the day in class. The more we **PRACTISE** a skill, such as learning to read and spell words or adding up numbers, the better we get at it.

Homework shouldn't take away from your play time and time with your family. It's best to find a time that works best for you and your family to get your homework done.

You may not have homework given to you very often at all, and that is okay. Every school is different, and every teacher is different – they may have other expectations of you.

Homework tips

- Find a COMFORTABLE, WELL-LIT area to do your homework, such as the dining table.
- Have a cup of WATER and maybe a HEALTHY SNACK with you, such as some cut up fruit.
- SET A TIME to complete your homework – it is not meant to take hours! If you are spending too much time on your homework, ask your parent or caregiver to let your teacher know that it is too much. (Don't worry! Your teacher will be perfectly fine with getting this message.)
- Have everything you need with you – e.g. pencils, eraser, worksheets, books.

What should I do if I don't understand my homework?

If you are having any trouble with your homework or don't understand what to do, ask a parent or care giver to help you (not to do it for you! ☺). You might also have a big brother or sister who can help you.

Don't **WORRY!**

Please don't let it worry you if you don't understand how to complete your homework. Just do what you can, and ask your parent to write a note to your teacher explaining that you are experiencing trouble. Lots of children find homework challenging at times.

Remember, when your teacher knows and understands that you are having difficulty, they can help make a **DIFFERENT PLAN** for you, so that you can have success!

Keep trying.

Just do your best.

what to do if...

(some common questions at school)

What to do if . . .

You are feeling sad or worried at school

If you are feeling SAD or WORRIED at school, make sure you tell your teacher. Your teacher will probably ask if you know what it is that you are worried about. Make sure you try to explain as best you can. Your teacher can help you better if they understand the full story and can offer some helpful support and suggestions.

You don't understand the work

There may be many times during your school years that you feel a bit CONFUSED or DON'T UNDERSTAND the work that you are doing in class.

Try to remember that the reason you attend school is to learn.

You are not expected to know or understand everything that your teacher explains.

I remember when I was at school, sometimes my teacher would have to explain how to complete a maths problem, or how to pronounce a tricky word, twice, three times or even MORE.

Don't ever worry about appearing silly if you don't understand something. The best thing you can do is ask your teacher to explain it again, and if you still don't understand, smile and ask again! Sometimes, you may want to ask a friend or a classmate sitting next to you to explain it to you. That might help too. But never worry about not understanding something. There is always someone around to help you out.

Other things you can try if you have trouble understanding in class...

WATCH Use eye contact – watch what your teacher is doing (try not to be distracted by things on your desk or what might be going on around you).

LISTEN Listen to what your teacher is saying and try not to talk while your teacher is giving instructions. You can't be talking and listening at exactly the same time.

ASK Ask for help if you don't understand instructions, and keep asking until you do!

You've forgotten your lunch box

If you get to school and realise you've left your lunch box at home, **DON'T PANIC!**

Tell your teacher so they are aware that you don't have your food with you. They can ask the lovely people who work in the school office to contact your parent or caregiver who may be able to drop it off at school. You may also have a good friend who might share a piece of fruit or sandwich with you. But please, make sure you talk to your teacher first. If you have any food allergies at all, you do not want to be sharing food.

You lose an item of clothing or toy at school

Many children lose all sorts of items at school. That is why we encourage you to **LABEL EVERYTHING** clearly with your name. It is very common for items of clothing to be left out in the playground, in another classroom, or in the gym.

Most schools have a designated area especially for lost property. It's a good idea to check the **LOST PROPERTY** first if you lose an item of clothing before looking elsewhere.

It's also a great idea to try and think back to the last place you might have been wearing that piece of clothing. There's a good chance that it is still there.

Finally, make sure you tell your teacher if you've lost something (and your parents too).

Usually, if a few people are on the lookout for your jacket, hat or jumper, it will find its way back to you – especially if it has your name on it!

DON'T BRING VALUABLE ITEMS TO SCHOOL! LEAVE THEM SAFELY AT HOME.

Someone takes something of yours

Sometimes at school, items that are important to you may go **MISSING**. That is why it is important that you have your name on all your possessions.

However, sometimes, friends or other students may make a choice to borrow or even take an item of yours without asking you.

It is **NOT** okay for another student to take an item of yours or to go through your school bag and other personal things. If this happens to you, let your teacher know and they will help you work this out.

If one of your school mates takes something of yours without asking you – such as your favourite pen, coloured pencils, book, ruler or food – you need to let them know, gently, that this is not okay.

Approach your friend / classmate and try this:

"Patrick, it's not okay for you to just take my pencil case without asking me. It is good manners to ask me first if you can borrow my things. This gives me the chance to say yes or no. Next time, please ask me."

If an item of yours has gone **MISSING**, and you don't know where it is, have a good look around before accusing someone of taking it. Check your locker, school bag, and under your desk again, just to make sure it isn't you who has misplaced the item.

If you **STILL** cannot find the lost item, let your teacher know. Sometimes in my own classroom, a student will come up the front to let me know that they have lost something – like a workbook, ruler or pen.

Sometimes, I ask the entire class to check their own things and take a look in their locker, just in case they mistakenly took the item. Mistakes **DO** happen, especially when there are many books and stationery items in the classroom at the one time.

Worrying does not take away tomorrow's troubles – it takes away today's peace.

unknown

Remember, your teacher is there to help if you can't solve the problem first by yourself. ☺

You are missing home

Especially in the first few days or weeks of starting school for the first time, you may feel a bit sad and miss being at home with your parents or caregiver. You may also be missing your friends from kinder if they haven't joined you at your new school.

Remember, starting primary school is a BIG change for you, and it is quite normal that you might be missing your parents or other carer during the day.

Perhaps you can pop a PHOTO of them in your school bag to take a look at during the day, or ask them to write you a little CARD that you can read when you might be missing them.

If you are feeling especially sad at school and missing home, quietly let your teacher know. They will be very used to other children feeling like this at times.

You are not the only one!

Your teacher might help you feel better by giving you a hug, finding something you can do to take your mind off how you are feeling, and finding some friends you can sit with to help you feel better.

It's okay to let your parents know that you felt SAD during the day, and that you MISSED THEM. They might have some other suggestions to help you get through those early days at school, too.

You get hurt in the playground

There will be times when you are busy playing in the playground, climbing on equipment, running around playing chasey, and an accident happens (just like they do at home).

If you get hurt, or have any problems while you are in the playground at recess or lunch time, look for the teacher or adult helper that is out on YARD DUTY. Usually, they will be wearing a brightly coloured vest so they will stand out.

If you can't find the yard duty teacher, take a friend with you up to the first aid room or the school office. Any adult will be able to help you get the medical attention you need.

You miss days of school

There will be times during primary school when unfortunately, you will get sick and won't be able to attend school for a day, or maybe many days in a row. You may feel worried or anxious that you will miss out on learning something important and feel behind on your work when you get back to school.

Please try not to **WORRY** about missing school if you are ill. Firstly, you **MUST** stay at home to **REST**, and let your body recover.

Secondly, staying away from school for a few days when you are unwell will also help to ensure that you don't pass on your illness (if it's contagious) to other classmates.

Don't worry!

YOU'LL BE BACK AMONG YOUR CLASSMATES AGAIN IN NO TIME.

There are also other events that might happen in the life of your family that may mean you have to take a day or more off from school. This might be when you have a **SPECIAL EVENT**, like a wedding, or a special family holiday. Your parents should let your teacher know if they know you are not going to be at school for any length of time.

If it's more than a few days, your teacher might make some arrangements with your parents to have you catch up on some important work missed at school.

Word find

S	U	N	G	A	B	L	O	O	H	C	S	R	O	U	T	I	N	E
A	L	S	U	N	H	A	T	F	O	L	K	O	O	B	N	S	T	Y
P	N	O	R	I	E	N	T	A	T	I	O	N	W	K	E	O	E	R
L	O	V	L	E	A	F	R	I	E	N	D	S	H	I	P	S	A	E
A	T	A	R	S	A	T	X	E	T	E	X	C	A	P	L	Y	C	N
Y	I	S	L	L	E	B	E	N	H	I	T	I	C	E	E	A	H	O
G	C	M	R	O	F	I	N	U	S	C	O	S	A	N	R	D	E	I
R	E	Y	O	U	C	T	O	S	N	S	A	S	M	C	A	I	R	T
O	S	N	H	A	R	T	R	U	L	E	R	O	P	I	S	L	Y	A
U	S	E	O	O	S	U	B	J	E	C	T	R	T	L	E	O	E	T
N	R	P	P	H	C	I	H	W	D	N	A	S	G	R	R	H	A	S
D	S	S	S	H	T	A	M	K	Z	O	B	M	O	V	A	L	R	T
L	U	N	C	H	B	O	X	E	L	T	T	O	B	R	E	T	A	W
H	O	M	E	W	O	R	K	Y	H	T	L	A	E	H	S	U	B	G

Circle these words as you find them (some may be backwards ☺)

camp	notices	orientation	pen
sunhat	waterbottle	friendship	pencil
teacher	schoolbag	oval	ruler
playground	lunchbox	sport	eraser
book	uniform	subject	scissors
textas	maths	art	stationery
bell	sandwhich	homework	healthy
routine	year	bus	holidays

Devices and the Internet

Being safe online

The internet is a wonderful place, filled with endless **INFORMATION**, **ENTERTAINMENT** and ways to **CONNECT** with your friends and family from all around the world!

Whatever age you are right now, I am sure that you know all about the internet, and will most likely be using computers, laptops and iPads at school and perhaps at home.

Did you know that when your parents were kids, they didn't even have the internet? Or if they did, they certainly couldn't do everything that you're able to do.

Ask:

- When you were my age, did you have computers?

  ___

- When did you use a computer for the first time?

  ___

- How did you communicate with your friends before the internet?

  ___

- When did you get your first mobile phone and what could you do with it?

  ___

- What do you think are the benefits of the internet today?

  ___

- What are some of the concerns you have about me having access to the internet today?

  ___

Of the many ways we use the internet, one of the main uses is to find out information. When you're at school and are given a project to do, you will likely be asked to **RESEARCH** a topic or person.

The easiest way to do this is by going onto your device (a laptop, computer, or iPad) and look it up in the search engine. But before the internet, children just like you had to go to their school or local public libraries to find books about that topic and take notes from there.

Some homes were lucky enough to have a collection of books called the '**ENCYCLOPEDIA**'. These books had thousands of pages that had information about any and every topic! But with the world changing as quickly as it is today, these encyclopaedias have become outdated.

If we use the internet to research a topic, it's important to use websites that are **OFFICIAL WEBSITES**, not just written by a person with an opinion.

Did you know that it's very easy for anyone to build a website and write things that may not be true? While researching on the internet can be very informative, we must always remember to check that the website comes from a reliable source.

Reliable websites

Here are some great websites that are guaranteed to provide you with reliable information for your next school project:

www.education.abc.net.au

www.natgeokids.com.au

www.worldwildlife.org

www.academickids.com

Rest and play time

Play

In primary school, you can get very busy – especially if you have out of school activities scheduled, along with homework. It's really important that you also have **TIME TO PLAY!** Even teenagers and adults need to make sure they schedule in time to do things they **ENJOY**.

What things do you like to do when you have time to play?

Perhaps you enjoy building **CUBBY HOUSES**, making **SLIME** or building things with **LEGO**.

When I was in primary school, I loved to play dress-ups, create plays with my best friend, and perform these in front of our friends and family. We also enjoyed playing with our dolls, and we would set them up and pretend we were teachers running a classroom.

There were other times when we played 'House' in my cubby, or we would set up a picnic in the backyard. If you have a few stuffed animals, you could pretend that you are the owner of a zoo and have the animals set up in different areas of your backyard. You could even make special signs for your zoo.

Use your imagination

Your imagination is **AMAZING** and can help you come up with many different play ideas.

School holidays

The school year is usually divided into four **TERMS**, each lasting between nine and eleven weeks. You then get to have a couple of weeks break for school holidays.

School holidays give you time out from the busy routine of school and give you the chance to sleep in, catch up with other friends, have play dates, relax and rest.

When summer time comes around, school will be over for the year. This break is **BIG** – up to 7 weeks off school!

This is a good opportunity to have family time and create many new memories. You may even be lucky enough to go on a holiday and travel to another town or state, or perhaps you'll just get to enjoy some fun time at home.

If you're at home and feeling a bit bored and missing school, why not try some of these ideas?

- Make play dough (with an adult's help) – see page 129.
- Plant a vegetable garden
- Write a children's book and create the illustrations
- Set up a tent outside and have a sleep out
- Build a cubby house inside using sheets and blankets (ask your parents first)
- Plant flowers in pots
- Clean out your wardrobe and donate any clothes that don't fit to charity.

More holiday ideas

- Have a cooking day
- Create some artwork
- Reorganise your bedroom
- Print out some favourite quotes for your bedroom wall
- Learn to knit or sew (ask an adult to teach you – maybe Grandma)
- Have a PJ day and watch your favourite movies with some popcorn
- Organise a sleepover with a school friend
- Read a book
- Listen to music
- Make up a dance
- Write a play with friends and perform it in front of your family
- Write a script for a short film and film it in your backyard
- Plan a picnic
- Visit the zoo
- Have a sleepover at your grandparents' house
- Build something with Lego
- Take photographs
- Make a kite out of sticks, paper and string
- Colour something in
- Build a volcano
- Make slime
- Bake and decorate cookies
- Lego challenges – build the highest tower
- Take a trip to the local library and borrow books
- Paint a large mural on a canvas
- Choose a spot on a map and ask mum or dad to take you on an adventure there
- Take a trip to the beach
- Go fishing
- Go hiking
- Draw paper dolls and cut them out
- Make sculptures out of clay
- Collect leaves and make artwork out of them
- Make play dough (see next page)

Making play dough

Time allowance – 40 minutes

YOU'LL NEED A HELPFUL ADULT TO ASSIST WITH THE SAUCEPAN ON THE STOVE

What you'll need

- ✔ Large saucepan
- ✔ Wooden spoon
- ✔ Small containers or zip-lock bags x 6

Ingredients

- ✔ 2 cups all-purpose flour
- ✔ ¾ cup salt
- ✔ 4 teaspoons cream of tartar
- ✔ 2 cups lukewarm water
- ✔ 2 tablespoons of vegetable oil (or coconut oil)
- ✔ Food colouring, optional

Method

- Mix together the flour, salt and cream of tartar in a large pot.
- Next add the water and oil. If you're only making one colour, add in the colour now as well.
- Cook over medium heat, stirring constantly. Continue stirring until the dough has thickened and begins to form into a ball.
- Remove from heat and then place onto wax paper. Allow to cool slightly and then knead until smooth.
- If you're adding colours after, divide the dough into balls (for how many colours you want) and then add the dough into small zip-lock bags or small containers.
- Begin with about 5 drops of colour and add more to brighten it. Knead the dough while inside the bag so it doesn't stain your hands. Once it's all mixed together, you're ready to PLAY.

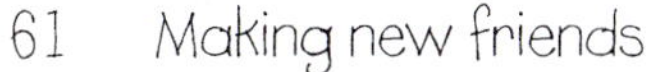

Hi there!

Welcome to GirlWise: a series of books that have been created especially for **YOU!**

This book has been written, especially to help you through the years that you will be moving through **PRIMARY SCHOOL**.

School can be a great time of learning new things, making friends, getting to know new teachers, playing lots of games, taking on new challenges, and learning to be part of a community.

School can also be tricky sometimes. Perhaps you feel a bit **NERVOUS** when you are faced with new situations. Or maybe, making new friends is hard for you. You may find it a little bit **SCARY** to be away from home during the day and you find yourself missing your parents.